THE UNOFFICIAL
WHOVIAN
RULE BOOK

A WIBBLY-WOBBLY, TIMEY-WIMEY
GUIDE TO AVOID DALEKS, CYBERMEN
& WEEPING ANGELS AND
SOMEWHAT COMPREHEND THE
TARDIS AND THE DOCTOR

By Duncan Levy

E-mail: info@thinkaha.com
20660 Stevens Creek Blvd., Suite 210
Cupertino, CA 95014

Published by THiNKaha®
20660 Stevens Creek Blvd., Suite 210, Cupertino, CA 95014
http://thinkaha.com

First Printing: April 2015
Paperback ISBN: 978-1-61699-151-7 (1-61699-151-8)
eBook ISBN: 978-1-61699-152-4 (1-61699-152-6)
Place of Publication: Silicon Valley, California, USA
Paperback Library of Congress Number: 2015904541

Trademarks

Warning and Disclaimer

Contents

A Wibbly-wobbly, Timey-wimey Guide . . .

Section I

General Rules

Whovians are the fans of the popular sci-fi show Doctor Who. They are the epitome of awesome, with good grammar and heightened knowledge that stems from their interest in space and time and information gained from many viewings of the show.

1

Rule 33: Alienating your friends until they watch Doctor Who is a necessary evil. Only then will they understand.

_____

_____

_____

2

Rule 50: Comparing everything to Doctor Who is completely normal and acceptable.

_____

_____

_____

3

Rule 115: "Wibbly-wobbly, timey-wimey" is an appropriate response to any question, and is not an arguable point.

_____

_____

_____

4

Rule 17: Until you became a Whovian, you'd never heard of "Trock" music. Now you can't get enough.

_____

_____

_____

5

Rule 69: It's DOCTOR Who, not Dr. Who. Never abbreviate Doctor!

_____

_____

_____

6

Rule 9: You must always stand and march when "I'm Gonna Be (500 Miles)" plays, and sing along with Whovians everywhere.

_____

_____

_____

7

Rule 147: It is perfectly acceptable to get your knowledge of history from the adventures of a 900-year-old Time Lord.

_____

_____

_____

8

Rule 150: Dreams are important. Never underestimate them.

_____

_____

_____

9

Rule 151: Rest is for the weary. Sleep is for the dead.

_____

_____

_____

10

Rule 152: Mobile phones have more uses than calling and texting (like engaging Cybermen emotions).

_____

_____

_____

11

Rule 160: It's perfectly acceptable to use the word "sonic" as a verb.

_____

_____

_____

12

Rule 176: Bad laws were made to be broken.

_____

_____

_____

13

Rule 180: First things first, but not
necessarily in that order.

_____

_____

_____

14

Rule 181: Logic merely enables one to be
wrong with authority.

_____

_____

_____

15

Rule 203: Never say, "Never ever."

_____

_____

_____

16

Rule 182: One may tolerate a world of demons for the sake of an angel.

_____

_____

_____

17

Rule 187: The one who makes fire is a leader.

_____

_____

_____

18

Rule 192: The Sonic Screwdriver may be harmless, but it's great at opening doors.

_____

_____

_____

19

Rule 196: You hate meeting non-Whovians. Describing Doctor Who makes you sound absurd.

_____

_____

_____

20

Rule 199: That feeling when you're watching a show or movie and they reference Doctor Who.

_____

_____

_____

21

Rule 202: Meeting up every ten years and swapping stories about caves is good fun. For a hermit.

_____

_____

_____

22

Rule 207: Fingers on lips is the best way to get a group's attention.

_____

_____

_____

23

Rule 208: When you have a secret that you can't tell anyone, simply say "Spoilers!"

_____

_____

_____

24

Rule 209: Take time to realize that peoples' faces can become them and they turn into something beautiful.

_____

_____

_____

25

Rule 210: Sometimes, Doctor Who is like foreshadowing in reverse. Don't worry, it will all make sense to everyone soon enough.

_____

_____

_____

Section II

The Doctor

Doctor Who is a British science-fiction television program produced by the BBC from 1963 to the present day. The program depicts the adventures of the Doctor, who is a Time Lord, a time-traveling humanoid alien.

Thirteen actors have so far headlined the series as the Doctor. The transition from one actor to another, and the differing approach to the role that they bring, is written into the show's plot as regeneration into a new incarnation, a life process of Time Lords through which the character of the Doctor takes on a new body and, to some extent, new personality, which occurs after sustaining injury that would be fatal to most other species.

26

Rule 1: The Doctor lies.

_____

_____

_____

27

Rule 116: "Go to your room" will always be terrible last words.

_____

_____

_____

28

Rule 120: All that I'll ever need to know in life, I have learned from Doctor Who.

_____

_____

_____

29

Rule 121: It's perfectly acceptable to look for a blue police box when you go outside.

_____

_____

_____

30

Rule 122: When something doesn't make sense, go poke it with a stick.

_____

_____

_____

31

Rule 138: The United Kingdom is where everything happens. EVERYTHING. American Whovians will always be annoyed by this.

_____

_____

_____

32

Rule 141: Everything has its time, and everything ends (even the run of your favorite Doctor).

_____

_____

_____

33

Rule 47: The Doctor's clothes are appropriate in any time and place.

_____

_____

_____

34

Rule 88: The best gift you can give is a bag
of air from your lungs.

_____

_____

_____

35

Rule 100: 3D glasses aren't for movies, they're for seeing Void Stuff.

_____

_____

_____

36

Rule 114: The Doctor doesn't look human. Humans look Time Lord.

_____

_____

_____

37

Rule 127: When wacky stuff is going on, the safest place is next to the Doctor.

_____

_____

_____

38

Rule 128: When in doubt, go barefoot; you'll look daft with just one shoe.

_____

_____

_____

39

Rule 146: Your lover may be the King of France, but the Doctor is the Lord of Time.

_____

_____

_____

40

Rule 157: Striped scarves, celery, Converse, bowties, fezzes and generally anything the Doctor wears will always be "cool."

_____

_____

_____

41

Rule 179: Anyone remotely interesting is mad in some way or another.

_____

_____

_____

42

Rule 170: The Doctor doesn't land on Sundays. Sundays are boring.

_____

_____

_____

43

Rule 165: If the celery turns purple, eat the celery. (If anything, surely it's good for your teeth.)

_____

_____

_____

44

Rule 191: Be highly suspicious when someone introduces themselves as John Smith.

_____

_____

_____

45

Rule 193: If you're attacking a man with a sonic screwdriver, don't let him near a sound system.

_____

_____

_____

46

Rule 194: The only lie the psychic paper can't handle is the notion that the Doctor is a responsible adult.

_____

_____

_____

47

Rule 206: There are some sentences the Doctor should stay away from.

_____

_____

_____

48

Rule 45: Always wear brainy specs. They make you look clever.

_____

_____

_____

49

Rule 35: The world doesn't end because the
Doctor dances.

_____

_____

_____

50

Rule 37: The Doctor is usually the first to argue with history.

_____

_____

_____

51

Rule 86: This man is "The Doctor" not "Doctor Who." Therefore, it is acceptable to correct others if they get it wrong.

_____

_____

_____

52

Rule 92: If the Doctor ever holds out his hand to you, you take it and you RUN!

_____

_____

_____

53

Rule 93: It is common courtesy, when put under arrest, to step into a police box and arrest yourself.

_____

_____

_____

54

Rule 101: "Well" is an appropriate response to almost any situation.

_____

_____

_____

55

Rule 164: The Master cannot kill the Doctor without humiliating him first.

_____

_____

_____

56

Rule 185: He's the Doctor, and if you don't like it and want to take it to a higher authority, there isn't one. It stops with him.

_____

_____

_____

A Wibbly-wobbly, Timey-wimey Guide ...

Section III

The TARDIS

The Doctor explores the universe in his TARDIS (Time and Relative Dimension in Space), a sentient time-traveling spaceship. Its exterior appears as a blue British police box, which is notably much larger on the inside than the outside and can blend in with its surroundings using the ship's "chameleon circuit."

Although "TARDIS" is a type of craft rather than a specific one, the Doctor's TARDIS is usually referred to as "the" TARDIS or, in some of the earlier serials, just as "the ship," "the blue box," "the capsule," or "the police box." It was already old when the Doctor first took it, but its actual age is not specified.

57

Rule 13: The TARDIS must always be called "Sexy" in private.

_____

_____

_____

58

Rule 16: TARDIS blue will become one of your favorite colors.

_____

_____

_____

59

Rule 26: The TARDIS isn't really supposed to make that noise. The Doctor just leaves the brakes on.

_____

_____

_____

60

Rule 89: It's okay to leave the TARDIS brakes on if they make a cool sound.

_____

_____

_____

61

Rule 195: The pretense of getting a key to the TARDIS gives anyone the time to run and save the Earth.

_____

_____

_____

Section IV

Companions

The Doctor's companions remind him of his "moral duty." His first companions seen on screen were his granddaughter, Susan Foreman (Carole Ann Ford), and her teachers, Barbara Wright (Jacqueline Hill) and Ian Chesterton (William Russell).

The Doctor regularly gains new companions and loses old ones; sometimes they return home or find new causes—or loves—on worlds they have visited. Some have died during the course of the series. Companions are usually human or humanoid aliens.

62

Rule 2: Doctor Who makes everything better except "Doomsday." That'll just make you feel worse.

_____

_____

_____

Section IV. a

Rose Tyler

63

Rule 23: It's okay to cry when you hear the word "canary".

_____

_____

_____

64

Rule 36: When the Doctor kissed the Matron in "Family of Blood", you still wished it was Rose.

_____

_____

_____

65

Rule 67: "I'm burning up a sun just to say goodbye" can be an acceptable replacement for "I love you."

_____

_____

_____

66

Rule 174: The name "Rose" can be fighting words when used as a threat.

_____

_____

_____

67

Rule 30: "Bad Wolf" is something much worse than a character from a fairy tale.

_____

_____

_____

Section IV. b

Mickey Smith

68

Rule 52: You still call Mickey, "the tin dog," even though he did turn into a BAMF.

_____

_____

_____

69

Rule 162: You CAN save the universe with a big yellow truck.

_____

_____

_____

70

Rule 163: You can learn to adequately fly a zeppelin on a PlayStation.

_____

_____

_____

71

Rule 171: Mickey may be the man in Havana and the technical support, but really, he's the tin dog.

_____

_____

_____

Section IV. c

Jack Harkness

72

Rule 19: Captain Jack no longer represents a pirate, but an immortal ex-Time Agent.

_____

_____

_____

73

Rule 55: Don't try to figure out how the Face
of Boe became only a head. It's a secret Jack
would never tell.

74

Rule 65: Being in total shock when you find out that Jack is the Face of Boe is completely normal.

_____

_____

_____

75

Rule 87: It's perfectly normal to be sexually frustrated after meeting Captain Jack Harkness.

_____

_____

_____

Section IV. d

Donna Noble

76

Rule 18: "Oi" will always remind you of the brilliant Donna Noble.

_____

_____

_____

77

Rule 24: Don't question it, just Turn Left.

_____

_____

_____

78

Rule 149: Donna's leaving of the Doctor will always be the saddest, because she will never remember her adventures.

_____

_____

_____

A Wibbly-wobbly, Timey-wimey Guide...

Section IV. e

River Song

79

Rule 11: Every plot hole can be plugged with the word "Spoilers."

_____

_____

_____

80

Rule 95: Killing people is wrong. Unless you're River Song.

_____

_____

_____

81

Rule 197: The language of the forest doesn't have a word for Pond. The only water in the forest is the River.

_____

_____

_____

A Wibbly-wobbly, Timey-wimey Guide . . .

Section IV. f

Amy Pond

82

Rule 135: Never trust mother-in-laws.

_____

_____

_____

83

Rule 159: It will always be the night before your wedding.

_____

_____

_____

Section IV. g

Torchwood

84

Rule 31: Torchwood is real. They produce Doctor Who to make audiences believe it is all fictional.

_____

_____

_____

Section V

Aliens

Doctor Who has a long list of fictional creatures, mostly aliens and extraterrestrials, from Daleks to Monoids, Sontarans, Urbankans, and many more. Monsters became a staple of Doctor Who almost from the beginning. The Doctor continues to battle against the most hideous evils in the universe.

85

Rule 20: Never blink when near a statue.

_____

_____

_____

86

Rule 27: There's nothing creepier than a weeping angel.

_____

_____

_____

87

Rule 56: The Statue of Liberty is a Weeping Angel, only she never moves because people are always looking at her.

_____

_____

_____

88

Rule 80: See a winged statue? Either a.) Don't blink, or b.) Fall to the ground crying, because let's face it. You don't stand a chance.

_____

_____

_____

89

Rule 103: Don't blink. Blink and you're dead.

_____

_____

_____

90

Rule 48: Stay out of the shadows.

_____

_____

_____

91

Rule 63: Always count the shadows. If it's double, you're dead.

_____

_____

_____

92

Rule 70: A library is a forest. Beware because the Vashta Nerada still live in its trees.

_____

_____

_____

93

Rule 51: It's okay to poke at the mannequins in the department stores. How else can you be sure that they are not Autons?

_____

_____

_____

94

Rule 62: Remember you can't shoot Sontarans.

_____

_____

_____

95

Rule 130: There are no appropriate safety measures against the Daleks.

_____

_____

_____

96

Rule 153: This is a "Dalek," not "Metaltron." (Wrong fandom.)

_____

_____

_____

97

Rule 154: Refusing to wear a Bluetooth because they look like Cybus Earpods is perfectly normal.

_____

_____

_____

98

Rule 158: They say to "never trust a nun, never trust a nurse, and never trust a cat." Beware the Sisters of Plentitude.

_____

_____

_____

A Wibbly-wobbly, Timey-wimey Guide . . .

Section VI

Actors

Thirteen actors have been introduced in the series as the Doctor. They transition from one actor to another as regeneration into a new incarnation, a life process of Time Lords through which the character of the Doctor takes on a new body and, to some extent, new personality, which occurs after sustaining injury that would be fatal to most other species.

While each actor's portrayal differs, they are all intended to be aspects of the same character, and form part of the same storyline. The time-traveling nature of the plot means that on occasion, story arcs have involved different Doctors meeting each other.

99

Rule 60: Christopher Eccleston will always be the most unappreciated Doctor.

_____

_____

_____

100

Rule 12: David Tennant in a kilt is one of the most erotic photos you will ever see.

_____

_____

_____

101

Rule 110: #SecretlyMarried. #MattSmith #KarenGillian

102

Rule 190: You get sad every time you remember Lis Sladen's passing.

103

Rule 198: The Doctor Who/Lauren Cooper sketch will cheer you up on the worst day.

_____

_____

_____

104

Rule 200: Favorite Whovian Game? "I spy people who have been on Doctor Who."

_____

_____

_____

105

Rule 5: Moffat is a Troll. In fact, he's King of the Trolls.

_____

_____

_____

106

Rule 7: "Moffat!" is an acceptable curse in some situations.

_____

_____

_____

107

Rule 34: The Moffat "Specials" are among some of the best.

_____

_____

_____

108

Rule 139: Trust in the Moff! He will not lead you astray!

_____

_____

_____

Section VII

Helpful Hints

Doctor Who is well-written, and its episodes provide an abundant source of stories from which to reference. From useful tips for survival, to inspirational quotes, Doctor Who is a perfect reference for all sorts of helpful advice.

109

Rule 105: Always bring a banana to a party.

_____

_____

_____

110

Rule 46: When you see cracks in the wall,
you'll probably want to scream and hide.

_____

_____

_____

111

Rule 53: Unopened fob watches will make
you rethink the word "fiction."

_____

_____

_____

112

Rule 61: If you're going to die, die looking like a Peruvian Folk Band.

_____

_____

_____

113

Rule 71: If you see something move in the mirror out of the corner of your eye, always assume it is Sister of Mine.

_____

_____

_____

114

Rule 72: Never underestimate the power of a Jammy Dodger.

_____

_____

_____

115

Rule 73: You can't let your mind wander when using psychic paper.

_____

_____

_____

116

Rule 84: You must always check the clocks when you enter a room to make sure they're the only thing ticking.

_____

_____

_____

117

Rule 22: Remember this: the Royal Family isn't exactly as they seem.

_____

_____

_____

118

Rule 107: Bendy straws add a little more fizz to any drink.

_____

_____

_____

119

Rule 81: Always waste time when you don't have any. Time is not the boss of you!

_____

_____

_____

120

Rule 169: Books are the best weapons in the world.

_____

_____

_____

121

Rule 134: Never ignore a coincidence. Unless you're busy, in which case, always ignore a coincidence.

_____

_____

_____

122

Rule 14: Don't wander off. Bad things happen when you wander off.

_____

_____

_____

123

Rule 184: They may shoot you dead, but you're good if you've got the moral high ground.

_____

_____

_____

A Wibbly-wobbly, Timey-wimey Guide . . .

Section VIII

Random Tidbits

Doctor Who is filled with random awesomeness, from the vast number and variety of enemies, to the design of their ships. Every aspect is different from any other show. While watching, you are sure to find an assortment of random facts and trivial knowledge to brighten your brain.

124

Rule 29: Being nice to the Doctor is not a prerequisite for surviving the episode.

_____

_____

_____

125

Rule 104: It doesn't matter if you're old, fat, and blue. If you owe the Doctor a favor, he will come to collect.

_____

_____

_____

126

Rule 111: Everyone knows who Harriet Jones is.

_____

_____

_____

127

Rule 132: Friends leave, but they're always your friends.

_____

_____

_____

128

Rule 137: There's always something to live for.

_____

_____

_____

129

Rule 155: A K-9 truly is a man's best friend.

_____

_____

_____

130

Rule 156: It's completely acceptable to be so emotionally invested in one-episode companions that you cry for days.

_____

_____

_____

131

Rule 201: Move over, Voldemort; Stormageddeon is dark lord of all.

_____

_____

_____

132

Rule 74: Hold tight and pretend it's a plan.

_____

_____

_____

133

Rule 85: Don't eat the snow. It could be Sycorax ash.

_____

_____

_____

134

Rule 97: Snow will always have you asking yourself, "What spaceship went and blew up in our atmosphere again?"

_____

_____

_____

135

Rule 129: You can hypnotize someone to walk like a chicken or sing like Elvis, but you can't hypnotize them to death.

136

Rule 167: If you require the services of the Doctor, make a Wish.

137

Rule 148: Spend a Christmas in London. It will increase your chances of meeting the Doctor.

_____

_____

_____

138

Rule 479: Be brilliant, and don't be afraid to say it.

_____

_____

_____

139

Rule 480: It's okay to wait a long time on someone if it's someone you love.

_____

_____

_____

140

Rule 68: 900 years of time and space and the Doctor has never met anyone who's not important. Have you?

_____

_____

_____

About the Author

Duncan Levy is 17 years old and is an even bigger fan of Doctor Who than Harry Potter (and has dressed up as The Doctor on multiple occasions). He loved the show and couldn't help but pull together a fraction of the best parts.